My Friend Rabbit

ERIC ROHMANN

SCHOLASTIC INC.

New York Toronto London Auckland Sydney
Mexico City New Delhi Hong Kong Buenos Aires

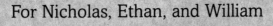

For Nicholas, Ethan, and William

ISBN 0-439-57683-0

12 11 10 9 8 7 6 5 4 3 2   3 4 5 6 7 8/0

Printed in Mexico   49

First Scholastic printing, September 2003

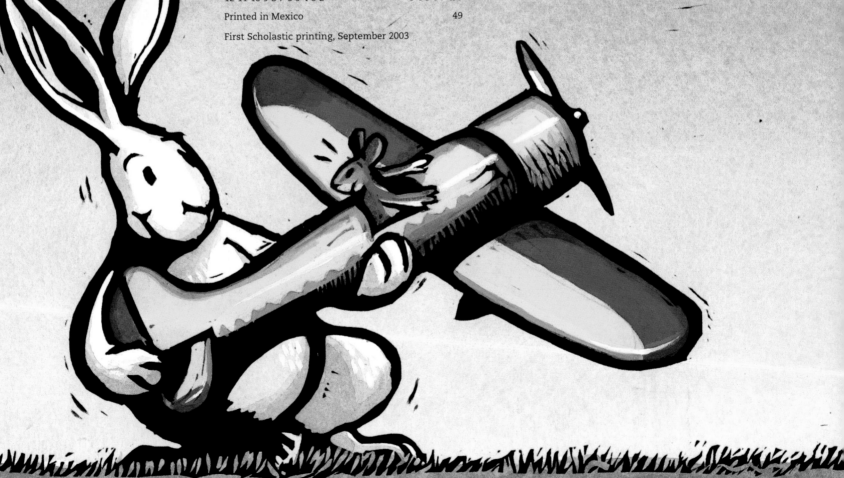

My friend Rabbit means well.
But whatever he does,
wherever he goes,

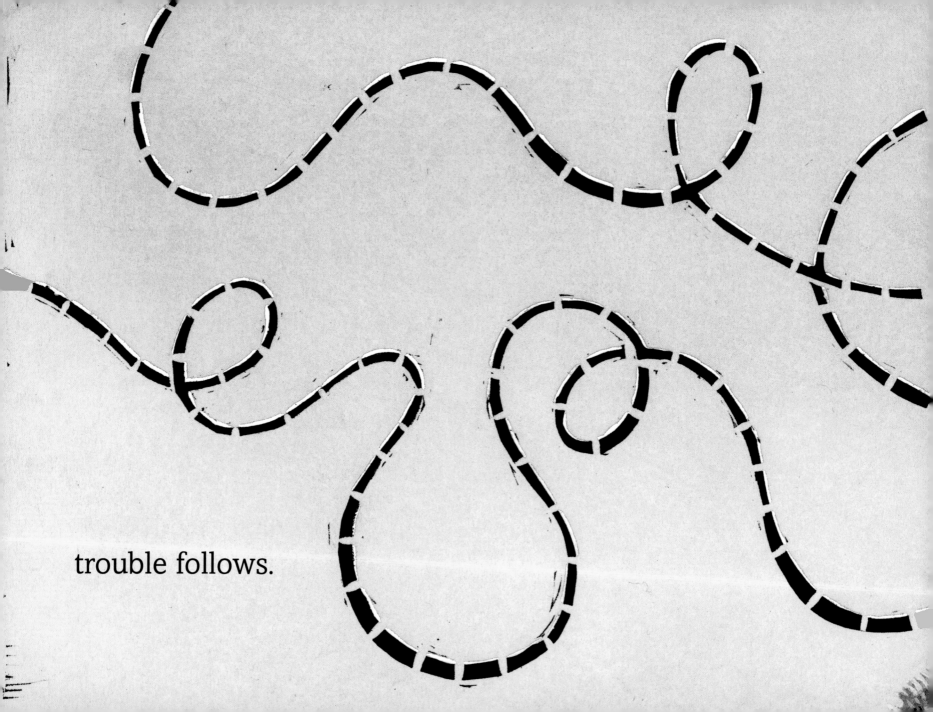

trouble follows.

"Not to worry, Mouse. I've got an idea!"

The plane was just out of reach. Rabbit said, "Not to worry, Mouse, I've got an idea."

So Rabbit held Squirrel
and Squirrel held me . . .

but then . . .

The animals were not happy.

But Rabbit means well.

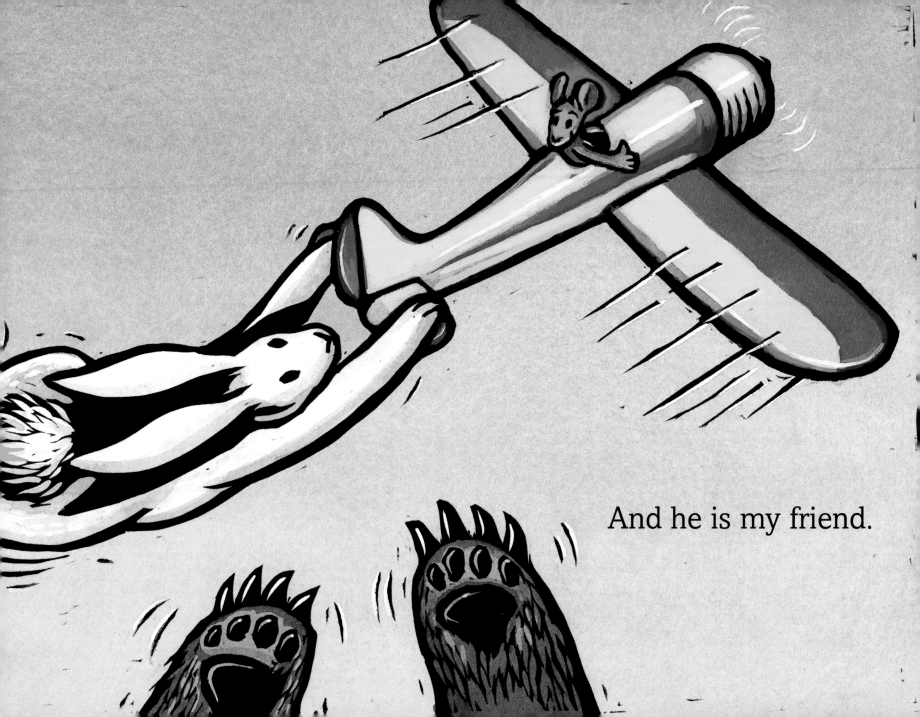

And he is my friend.

Even if, whatever he does,

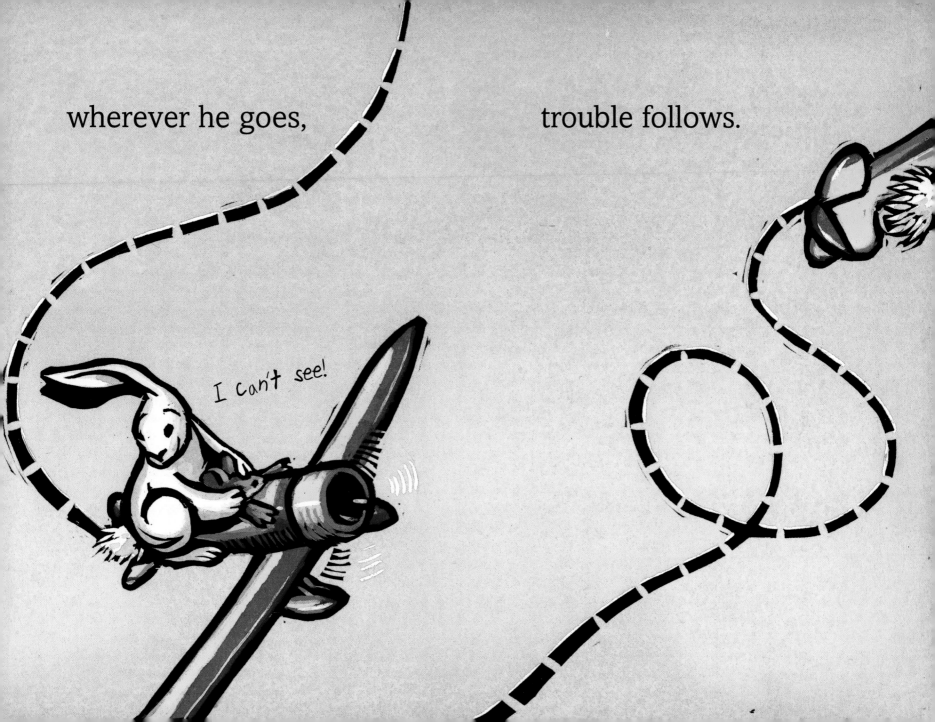

"Not to worry, Mouse,
    I've got an idea."